Clever Fox Press Ltd
www.cleverfoxpress.org

Ordering Information:

Quantity sales. Special discounts are available
on quantity purchases by corporations, associations,
and others. For details, contact the publisher
at the address above.

Orders by trade bookstores and wholesalers,
please contact julie@cleverfoxpress.com

Publisher's Cataloguing-in-Publication data
Fuxman, Shelly

My Messy Mind / Shelly Fuxman

Poetry

First Edition

My Messy Mind

Poetry Collection

by
Shelly Fuxman

A Bad Poem

A poem is bad when it makes sense.
Hence, I write with a quasi-illiterate style
And nobody understands me, all the while.

A Peculiar Family

Hourglass

It was a picture of him.
In black and white
His skin looked velvet.

Walking along the edge of the water.
He picked up seashells
And kept them in a box by my bed
Because they resembled my name.

We climbed fences,
jumped over walls
Just because.

When we sat on the right side of things
We would stare at the sun rippling on the water.

We would only ever spend time on that beach,
grass was too green for him,
Much too boring.

It makes me cry
That I can't remember
How tiny hands
Fit in rough palms.

Maybe I was Right

I thought banks gave out money to the poor.
Maybe I was right.
They press buttons that sing songs in puzzles then they
smile because they won a cash prize.
I thought, why did Daddy work so hard if banks gave
money to the poor.
Daddy said we're not poor enough. Maybe he was right.
I waited.
I thought why didn't I see Daddy if banks gave money
to the poor.
I thought Daddy was the bank and gave all our money
to the poor.
Maybe I was right.
I thought why did Daddy yell at Mummy when she cut
price tags off.
And how come Daddy has blue wrinkles under his eyes.
I took Daddy to the bank and told him now we're poor.
And he said you're right.
Daddy lost the game.
I picked up a penny from the pavement
And put it in his pocket.

Mouse

No, I didn't touch the mouse
I picked it up from its tail

No, I didn't touch the doorknob
I opened it with my knees
And placed the mouse on a wet leaf

I washed my hands

You told me not to save its life
You said what was the point
You screamed in disgust when
You saw me bend down to it.

My house is broken.
You didn't tell me that,
I figured it out
From the way you looked at it.
Chased after it
Bit it
And then carried it in your teeth.

I have made no difference.

My Wandering Mind

I lost my pink bunny rabbit teddy
In the tiny bed of the place I used to call home.
I lost my angel
They said she was stolen by a reckless driver.
I lost my mother to an orange plastic bottle.
She stopped crying
I lost my father to his glasses.

That night
On the roof, cold, I was just staring up
But they pulled me in by my arms
I stumbled
I answered "No"
I tore my throat
I was pulled unwilling by the sleeves of my shirt,
ripped up the stairs
I screamed "I'm broken, I'm broken don't you get it?
You won."

And just like that I lost myself.

Overindulgence (Consequences)

Did you know that drinking with friends on holidays
in foreign countries leads to drunkenness which leads
to mistakes which lead to hospitals which lead to death?

Did you know that tattoos on drunken holidays in
foreign countries lead to pain which leads to blood
infections which lead to hospitals which lead to death?

Did you know that sex with strangers on drunken
holidays in foreign countries leads to pregnancy
which leads to babies which lead to death?

Did you know that eating on drunken holidays leads
to food poisoning which leads to throwing up which
leads to hospitals which lead to death?

Maybe I should go on a health retreat with my mother.

Plastic Hands

The instructions, in small print on the back of the box,
Tell me it has to be fed Playdoh chunks
Three times a day.

The string is pulled and it tells the same joke
Seven times.

Sometimes I cover its rubber mouth with my hand and wait.
See how long it can breathe for.
When I remember it's not real
I take off my hand and
Hope its eyes will close.

With a government supplied recording device
On the left side of its chest
It tells my secrets:
The stolen alcohol
The scratches on its shins
Its little crib that wasn't made.

It doesn't lift a finger
It can't they're stuck together
In plastic hands.

Because it doesn't speak until spoken to
The master of the house picked it as his own.
And I run in circles
Making its limbs move.

I drag it out to bus seats and coffees in shitty cafés.
It doesn't shout.
It doesn't cry.
It just waits and somehow learns
To walk up stairs and close doors.

Pig Mum

She wears these brown leggings which make her look
almost as if she were half-dipped in mud. And she doesn't
see it.
In fact, she only ever looks at her face.
She stopped looking down at herself when she could
look down at her piglet instead.
"Poor, stupid piglet," she would say, "why can't you be
as happy as I am?"

She eats unashamed like a pig, from her fingers to her
mouth.
That's why she didn't understand why her piglet didn't
want to any more.
But despite her whiskers she loved her litter
And she hummed to them as they lay beside her.

She didn't marry well, to be perfectly honest,
So they only sleep on a dew soaked patch of muddied hay.
But it was enough for her.
She didn't strive for more.

And though she pushed her little piglet too hard,
Too soon to stand up on her own four trotters,
Though she dreamed a little too big,
She was sorry.

Or, at least, as sorry as a pig could be.

Purple Nails

I'm sure that you wouldn't be too surprised
If I told you that,
When I think of your hands,
I see them poised and relaxed
Holding a gossip-filled magazine,
Steadily and delicately
Flipping the thin pages.
I would call them wrinkly
But it would leave
A hand-shaped pink mark
On my right cheek.
The nails are never lacking
In a blindingly bright colour:
Fluorescent purple,
Acrylic red,
Anything that took your fancy.
Rather reluctantly,
They would put down the magazine
For another coat to be added
While someone behind you was doing your hair
And someone in front massaging your feet.
You always loved to be treated like a queen.
You demanded it.
And with the flick of your wrist
Your humble servants obeyed.
I, your loyal subject,
Translated broken English
As your hands skimmed
Through clothing sizes and bag options.

Talking to Walls

You picked up a conversation and threw it in my face
You spat false facts
I screamed.

When you got tired
you told me I was wrong.

With one hand you picked up the phone
With the other you held my throat
And you told me the conversation was over
I couldn't even reply.

You let go and paced
Back and forth
Waiting for me
To erupt
And have no chance to cry.

You laughed
You twisted your own words
Then, you waited.

The Unfathomable

I'm truly perplexed
At the unfathomable thought
That you, dearest,
Who has always been so much there
(At times in distance waving
At times too close, breathing down my neck)
Will soon not be here.

Of course the memories,
Which I hope will never blur
Over the un-reminded years,
Will always keep you somewhat alive.
But I can't really imagine it.
At least I don't think I will be able to
Until —

I have told myself that
One day I will be ready
And it won't hurt too much
If I carry on sipping
From a bottle of wine from my bedside.

You Held the Paint Brush

You held the paint brush while I held the marker.
You started the picture but I always messed it up.
You placed the sequins and I poured over the glitter.
You held the artwork but I spilled the glue.
You said it was perfect.

But now,
The imperfections are wrong.
And everything I do is wrong and everywhere I go is wrong.
I just couldn't do it the way that you did. I never could.
Because the paint brushes and the markers are scattered
on the table.
The glitter and glue have clumped on the pages.
All the pictures are torn, misshapen and water-stained.
Because you're not here.

Creations

A Night-time Symphony

My curtains were only slightly open

I could only see the shadow of his headlights as it
Coloured the walls of my room
From one side to another,
Danced across my pictures,
Lit up the leaves.
It didn't disturb the night-time peace, it just illuminated it.

No, the birds were chirping
And the draught whistled in harmony.

No, a woman began shouting into her phone.
"They're not crazy, I am," and
"I have too many lemons in my fridge."

The sound of trees is starting to irritate me.

My window slammed shut.
My curtains stood still.
All stood still.

A Painting

A rich streak of bright azure paint
From left to right
Unblemished
Fading as it goes
To a soft grey.
Almost unnoticeable.
The hilly horizon, holding it all, is freckled with vineyards
And innumerable trees
And villas
With weaving golden strokes of path.

But that is in the distance.

A maze of tiled roofs
Of clay and auburn burnt by the sun.
Every little street too narrow.
And the lives of each Mediterranean spilled through
the windows
With the smell of sunlight, fresh bread and jamón.

Apple Cheeks

I noticed that the sun hurts to look at
And the bees hum so loud.
I understood why people hate it when I sing.

I noticed that the sky is exactly the same as it used to be
And that smell too.

It's almost exactly the same
But just so not the same because
I feel it more;
I reminisce;
I even cry a little.

Because it's gone.

Then, I smiled at the sun,
Let it greet my apple cheeks
And sipped from a juice box straw.

Boredom Strikes

When boredom strikes,
I stare into each one of my teddy bears' eyes and
shout their names at their stupid faces.
I grab my family's shoes and throw them on
the neighbour's tree.
And vice versa.
I pet my cats until I have their fur.
I try their food off their plates.
I sit in the closet and scream my throat raw.
I pee in the toilet like a man.
I pee next to the toilet like a man.
I sit on tables and fine dine off chairs.
I hold my breath and wait.

Butterfly

When it all disappeared
I unpinned a butterfly from the wall
And pulled at its wings so it would fly.
My pen tip touched a piece of paper,
And I saw it again.
Words on paper in books
Sprouting flowers and leaves
Like dog-eared pages.

Green

It was inside me.
In my hair, under the soles of my feet.

I smashed my head into a red-brick wall.
One with a concrete cross on it.
I smiled and everyone admired.
My beautiful complexity drew him in.
I told him to "fuck off."
He said he would be happy to.
I waved my hand across his face.
I told him not to touch me
And he didn't even though I was leaving.

He won. He smiled as he held my mother's bleeding
hands
And as her life suddenly fell
He made me cry in a car filled with suitcases.

Then, it slammed the door.
My mother's favourite colour was green.

He (with a Capital H)

Thusly, he enslaves his people
And watches them struggle for his heaven.
Jacob's ladder always ascends to
A gold-plated gate surrounded by babies with stapled
on wings,
soft suede cheeks,
Completely nude.

In fact, He made Michelangelo his favourite son
To paint them for the rich
On their walls and ceilings.

And If you play by His rules
The gates open as if by magic
And some of Santa's elves
And the population
Is six.

I Hate Boats

I
I don't belong here.
I can't breathe.
I can't do this.

I'm tired of crying,
thinking.
I'm tired.

I hate that word "No"
Coming from your mouth.
You are ruining my life.

II
Somehow, I'm still here.
Nauseous.

I'm too scared of dying
Or scared to be the only one living,
Scared to leave possessions behind.
I wonder if I can drown the toddler and keep my suitcase.

I am told I have to smile.
They're so different.
They seem happy.

III
The mast stood looking at the sunset.
It never turned around;
It just looked at the horizon
Where sea and sky make mountains grow
Grey melts
Unsteady, dark, freckled.
Salty and blurred air.
My eyes grow weak; his do not.

Isn't this where murders and romances happen?
I'll sit and wait for either.

IV
The sky is one colour now and I am inside it.

My mast.
I can't see his face.

Turn around.
If you don't I'll cry again.
You make me sick
The way your passions
take over you
when you look into
Broken water...

It's trapped too.
I don't blink.

V
The black is moving.
I'm breathing.

I told myself to wait
For stars.
I would sleep here, waiting.
Don't move me.

I am a child, remember?
A child who grew up too tall
For tears,
Too old
To hold her mother's hand,
Spent too much time here
To cry again.

VI
Oh look, the stars!
I didn't see you come in.
Don't look at me like that,
I'm trying not to cry.
I promise
I'm smiling,
It's just that
My lips taste like salt.

VII
This cannot wait until the morning:

Two women glow
in the distance:
One unbothered by age;
The other young
but turned away
for she does not know how much beauty has graced her.

"Turn around"
The water echoes.
It would have been surreal.

VIII
The wind is too strong now.

He spits,
Pulls my hair,
My eyes,
I can't sleep in turmoil.
Ropes drag against metal.
That's the warning call.

I wait.
I'll go now.

IX
The water is cold
But it's so clear that
When it laughs
Its teeth hurt.

Empty skyed,
I will float here for the rest of the day.
Just see where I will go.
I don't need to speak.

Nobody will know
Where she went.

X
Everyone is gone.

If it could stay like this.
If I could burn to caramel
In the white sun
With dotted white houses.

Aloneness and peace just smiling.
I hear music.
The sound of water.

I think I belong here.

It

From one side of the landscape to the other
It walked with long and slender legs
Beside the Mediterranean Sea,
Gnawing at the edge of the shore.
It had its chin up and its head
Was level with dignity and confidence.
Its mane fluttered
Like a golden cape in the breeze.
Its body was thin, caramel-coloured
And effortlessly immaculate.
Even the sun, on setting, shone its light
For all to see the impossible beauty.
Blue eyes pierced the hearts of every man alive.
And they were hers.

Mother Nature is an Illusionist

Scattering bugs
Among towering grass blades
Weaving in and out of tangled roots.
"They're more scared of you than you are of them."

Trunks of trees stretched up
And fanned out
Twisting branches.
The sky is torn apart by nodding,
Circling leaves in the breeze.
The sun is reaching down.
"Let's sit in the shade over there."

The waterfall fed the river.

"Yes, those are the birds chirping."
"No, dear, they're not doing that to piss you off."

Reality

The bubbles fizzle out,
The candles run out of wax,
The music stops playing;
Silence.
Except for the draining of murky water
And heavy breathing.

Spilling the Tea

When I was angry
I was told "Don't shout"
I was told "Drink tea"
And "wait before you drink it"
And "burn yourself to learn that
Mistakes are like your lovers.
The ones disapproved of,
The ones you remember the most."
I was told to "Remember
That you are what they see
But don't let it burn you"
And
"Cry. But then stop you're wasting time."
"Cry. But then stop that's enough now."
"Cry. No, stop.
You're getting my shoulder wet."

The Delingqwent Inside

The delingqwent inside wants to take a trip to Oxford
or Cambridge
To piss on their vast green lawns.

She wants to shout obscenities in lecture halls
Create a scandal: mix up the names of German
Philosophers
She wants to stare at clock numbers, run out of empty
classrooms etc. etc.
Make fun of names of doctors without the auditorium
turning. Staring. Waiting.

She can't hold her train of thought.
She wants people to put the fuck down their Shakespeare
And pick up a shitty lollipop from a paediatrician's office
And suck it until the paper falls apart in the mouth.
Is that too much to ask for?

To the Uninvited Guest

To you,
I am invisible,
Until, of course, it is most convenient.
Then, I am blocking your vision.

To you,
I am mute
Until, of course, I am mistaken.
Then I am too loud.

But to me,
Your transparent smiles lie.
But, of course, I believe you
Because you gave me no choice.

So to them,
I can only hope I am more enough
Than I ever was for you.
Even with a raw throat, wet eyes and bleeding.

Too Busy

The kids are barking,
The dog is crying,
My husband needs to be cooked,
The dinner won't help me,
The dishwasher is complaining,
My mother-in-law broke.
I'm tired.
And my glass of wine just overflowed.

Lola

Chocolate

Thank you for showing me
That I can't be scared of anything else now
That empty lined paper in silent rooms doesn't matter
That my mistakes really make no difference.

Thank you for hiding yourself before I could see you
For keeping yourself by that window
Keeping your eyes open.

Thank you for tears and sympathies
I begged my pillowcase I would never have.
Now the ones I love are in my back teeth
And I eat chocolate so they smile.

Thank you for leaving
And for leaving her behind.
She has your nose.

Common Knowledge

It is widely known that the woman two doors down has a
black and white cat she calls bubbles and bubbles can
only look through some windows.
It is widely known that this is because I was run over and
killed by a car with an empty driver's seat.
It is widely known that no one came to our door and rang
the doorbell (he must have known it was broken).
It is widely known that I am still lying between the yellow
lines.
It is widely known that my family didn't want the ashes
And the mourning stopped after a day.

My brother didn't even cry.

Instructions for Not Becoming a Cat

First you start to feel a little lethargic
Suddenly the thought of mice excites you
And you get the urge to... lick yourself.

Don't.

Avoid risky situations.

When fatigued after a long day of doing absolutely
nothing,
Stay clear of comfortable places:
Dilapidated couches, cushions, people's faces.

When entranced by the thought of swinging shoelaces:
Take deep breaths
Think vacuum cleaner.

And if you finished your plate but you're still feeling
peckish
Resist shouting at others for more.

That's not how you make friends.

Lola

I've always wondered
Why many call you
'Untimely'
When I've never
Seen you be
Timely.

You've never been
Un-cried for
You've never been
Un-hated for
You've never
Un-touched anyone.

And you took her
From my hands
Onto yours.
You hurt me
So much more than anyone else has.
In fact, I never thought that I could hurt just this much.

So.
Now I am scared of
your good friend
Time.
Because when Time runs out
You're there.
Waving, beaming.

And when she ran
And when she stopped running
Because she couldn't run anymore
And she loved to run

I don't really understand it all yet.

No One Even Cried

She walked along a string embroidered with autumn
leaves pursued by men who lost their balance and fell off
along the way.
She stopped; she turned.
A sign said 'I hate you'
And she was bleeding from her belly button.
No one even cried because the flowers were turning pink
and purple,
The sun rested on puddles - trees and lampposts grew.
And she forgot how to kiss
And she forgot how to love
And she couldn't see her eyes in mirrors.

Then somebody cut the string.

Love?

A Fairy-tale Ending

There are children climbing out of tombs
A princess reading a fairy tale
Prince charming is drunk.
Staring through her at the wall.

When his child dies of starvation
He will miss her more
Because a child is the only thing that keeps them
beautiful.
In the clinical light of a therapist's office
They're puppets in the hands of text books.

They might not make it out of their four-poster bed
tonight.

A Heavy Love

I found someone who didn't mind too much holding
my hand
Who didn't mind too much holding my weight
My head on their velvet arm.

I thought we flew

I thought we flew so much that the wind blew her hair
To perfectly cascade onto her shoulders
And made red dress hug her.

Her eyes shimmered
Her perfection was too much to give up on someone
Who let herself rest her head.
I understand now it was too heavy.

I watched you drift into her.
I let you.

An Option

Nothing hurts like watching someone
You once thought you knew
Walk out the door
Turn their back
As if
You were
Just one person
Out of so many options.
That you were just one stop
Just one broken door.

Crying at a Statue of Him

I hate this, the gap.
I don't usually swallow the hurt.
I promised myself to be strong.
Hold my eyes somewhere else.
I even changed my smile.

But.
How was I supposed to pretend I couldn't feel her?

Or ask
Do you want to just start again?
Pretend that nothing happened?
Or are you afraid that if you look into my eyes
That you will start to feel what we told ourselves we can't?
Or that suddenly it would all just fall into place
and we would realise that we were wrong to let go
and that we were meant to be together
Or perhaps somehow we could maybe even make things
work
in some ridiculously perfect way.

I promised myself I would not cry at your cold feet.

Drunk and Smokey

As I sit here, staring at the rippled ceiling
All I want to do
Is throw my pride onto the coffee table
There with the overturned empty bottles and cigarette
butts and write
I miss you
A hundred times over
And wait for you to read it
And not reply
Or wait for you to
Reply that it's too late for us
That too much has been broken
That we can't go back to the sweet, unruined beginning

But
When my eyes turn to the door
I remember
It was you
Who closed your ears to my singing
And you who should be picking up the phone
In a flurry of emotion
Begging
To go back
To that unstained start.

The one that you stepped on.

Dying

I started dying when I learned your full name
I started dying when I put it next to mine
I started dying when you changed your mind
I started dying when we walked through the park
I started dying when my mother didn't like you;
my friends turned their backs
I started dying when you held your breath
I started dying when you took my hand
I started dying when you said thank you;
when you made that joke
I started dying when the first tear came
I started dying when the elevator door closed
I started dying when you taught me heartbreak
I started dying when I heard new names
I started dying when you were happy.

Glow

He liked the way I glowed in his right hand
The way he could toss me out like ashes at the end
of his cigarette
And then breathe me in until I was nothing.

But I liked sitting in between his two fingers
Being tasted with wine
And waiting to be stubbed out on the arm of his couch.

His Jewel

A jewel sits silent beside a silver chain.

Such a beauty must belong to
Someone.
Someone royal,
Someone just as hypnotising in the light.

He hangs the chain around her neck.
"Too tight?"
She can't breathe.
"Perfect".

She is so beautiful and so fortunate, is she not?
She smiles.
Her eyes glimmer too.
The epitome of grace.

How to Stay Single

I was told by the man across the table that I need
to stop wikipediaing my way into people's hearts
I was told that I'm bad at not talking about my cat
That I'm bad at seeming nonchalant
I was told that I feel things too much
I look into the eyes too much.

I told the waiter what I wanted to eat — too much,
by the look in his eyes
I was told that I should not call the waiter by their first name
So I said: "Well, Chris the waiter. I suppose now
we'll be *waiting* on you"
I was told I need to be a dad to make jokes like those.

Well, we did the cheque dance; he won.
He walked me back to door 33,
And, intimidated by my cat's impatient eyes,
Left with a cold kiss on the cheek
To discuss the events with my good friends Ben and Jerry.

If Love were a Table

I've seen this table.
She is soft-brown in complexion.
Her legs are long, slender and curvaceous.
A crimson cloth has thrown itself across her.
She has scratches, she has dents and she has Chinese
take-out food stains.
A candle rests at her centre, solitary but glowing, but
there is no rose.
She doesn't need one.
Two chairs, two plates, two forks, two knives, two glasses.
One bottle of red.

Maybe it's the Wine

The feeling when you look into someone's eyes
And you know.
The feeling when you both smile
And you know.
You know the feeling
when everything is so different
yet exactly the same?
It clicks;
Sparks fly.
But maybe it's the wine.

Messy Politics

Broken Signs

Ash like glitter sparkles above me.
With rose-tinted glasses the sky looks pink.
Or just darker.

The ground cuts.
It didn't want me here anymore.

I can't hear much through the music in my head.
I try to breathe to it.

As the broken signs wave, I waved back.
Everyone is leaving but I don't want to.
Why would I leave my home?

I wasn't on the ground anymore.
But now, at least, my night light was shining again.
Red, blue, red, blue.
Black.

Fine Dining

Women who hold their breath at dining-room tables
Because their chair legs aren't tall enough.

Women who hold their breath at dining-room tables
Because the porcelain dolls are watching.

Women who hold their breath at dining-room tables
Because she's just so lucky.

Women who hold their breath at dining-room tables
Because "Oh, no don't say that you'll only frighten him
away."

Women who hold their breath at dining-room tables
Because Wordsworth fills the silence.

Women who hold their breath at dining-room tables
Because a guest never complains.

I was a Witness

I saw you that day.
I was a witness to what you did.
To me, to her,
To anyone you could reach.
I assume you don't know how to respond to
Woman.
So you stopped the clock, reversed it
Somehow.
Because you could.
But they don't believe me —
Not even under the blinding lights,
Not even under watery eyes,
Not even under oath.
But I was there.
I was a witness.

Mr Misogynist

I take Mr Misogynist to a fancy restaurant.
A waitress serves us drinks.
"You like that don't you, being served" I joke.

I suggest Mr Misogynist a detour to a garden centre.
He admires the bushes for far too long.
"What are you thinking about?"
He tries to laugh.

I lose at noughts and crosses.
"Must be because I have a vagina" I joke again.
He nods and draws a line through three O's.

I question his views on racial prejudice.
"Surprisingly liberal for a misogynist."
He laughs too hard.

I offered Mr Misogynist a ride home.
He decided to drive my car.
"The wheel is yours," I said.
"Wouldn't want to be hospitalised on such a lovely day."
He opened my door first.

I asked Mr Misogynist if there's a Mrs Misogynist.
He said she was out of town for a couple of days
And gave me a tour of his bedroom.

Statuesque

She formed a statue
Now looking more like a husk
Someone had painted her gold
Just enough to cover the rust
But too much to stop her lips from parting.
Her veins were blocked
Her cheeks untinctured
Her eyes looked ahead
As if there was something there
Some hope.
And on the plaque,
Beneath her hardened feet
Announced
"Woman" as created by man.

"They're not Humans, They're Animals!"

"They're not humans, they're animals!"
It's foolish to entertain such conversations with white walls.

"They're harassing you; can't you see?"
"You're boring me."

The leaves are starting to fall.

Like apes, they ask me how my day has been.
Because they weren't listening, they say: "Pardon?"
And tip pink Himalayan salt into my glass.

It's just that I don't know who is real anymore:
The ones shouting their truth at my face
Or those denying it on their high horse.

Literally.

Self-Love

–

Self-Loathe

A Tragedy

To myself, I apologise
Because what I want to be, I synthesise

I often let my imagination run away
I feel those feelings often considered cliché

As if these thoughts I could romanticise
Yet in truth so much by heart I cannot memorise

Then I lost my audience because the critics said I overplay
That my life is not a performance in a night-time cabaret

They tell me then my show has no reprise
So I must now begin to 'un-dramatise'

And as on this stage my welcome I seem to overstay.
I put my feathered quill and scroll away

Then I call myself for the finishing bow
And bid my adieus to ye faithful readers now.

Bathing in Grief

I'm washing out my problems until my skin turns raw
And soaking them back in
Until my skin wrinkles
And spits me out

On following a path of landmarks
With my finger
Through the bubbles
I've realised that
The reflection in the running faucet
Is not my own
That the name they say I suit
Is not my own
But one given to me.

I see my hair around me
Cutting the white ceramic
Like pure white
could ooze into the water
And harden
Fix me here, now
So I can stop being able to hurt.

Different

I don't know quite what it is but
It made something different
I doubted more,
No, I wasn't sure what to doubt.

The skin under my eyes changed.
It made them soft and blue and stretch down to my cheeks.
It growled when I sighed.
It sighed when I growled.
We were made for each other.

The sun started drowning
I started crying; I just killed it faster.
Maybe now it will whimper and know
What my pen knows.
The air, somehow, became crisp with
Its condensing breath and
We shared it
Sipping on plastic straws.

Ghosts

They picked me.
They flip the calendar pages so all I see is numbers of
days of months
But I can't do the maths so I lose my place.
They toy with the food on my plate
And I don't know why
But I start crying in front of strangers
At Pret a Manger.
They used to steal my teeth so I never met the tooth fairy.
They stole my cat.
Mugs stack up in the corners of my room leaving rings
on the table or tea stains along the edges where their lips
touch.
They make mirrors appear of two-sided glass.

"No, of course they're not real.
I just feel things too much."

I am a Disgrace

My hair was coming out of the top of my head
So it would heavily obstruct my vision if the wind were
to blow
As it would on an average English afternoon.

I figured I shouldn't go out for the day
Because each of my hands had five fingers which everyone
would see
If I were to wave hello to someone.

I didn't want to bear the thought of people seeing me
With two lips (top and bottom) and two eyes (left and right)
An uncanny resemblance to my mother.

And just the thought of someone seeing my nose
Right in the middle of my face!
Why would I want to parade around the fact that I have
a sense of smell?
I am disgrace.
I can't go out in public looking like this!

They will look at me
And they will judge me
And I will come back home
And I will cry
Because all I wanted was some semi-skimmed milk from
Sainsbury's.

In the Details

I told him that I believed my name wasn't my own
But one given to me like mismatched buttons on a worn-
out sweater.
In fact when people call me by my name I don't turn
around any more.
I told him to not call me by my name but by my
imperfections,
The ones that I thought everyone could see. The ones my
mirror saw.

So one by one he said them, listed them, wrote them out
on a notepad with a blunt pencil so he wouldn't forget
that my belly was brimming my jeans, my skin blemished,
my hair mussed, my nose large, my nails cracked, my legs
short, my thighs fat, my chest too small, my eyes brown,
my narcissism too... well... narcissistic.

I turned around teary eyed, smiling.
"Thank you for noticing," I said,
"I thought it was just me."

Metamorphosis

Would you still love me If I let my eyebrows grow into one
If I let my arms and legs grow forests
Let my hair turn grey

Would you still want me if I lost the colour in my eyes
If I lost my smile
Just had wrinkles cutting my cheeks

Would you stay if my tears became salty
My nails stubs, my lips dry
My scars left red
My skin left loose
The bags under my eyes left to drip
Down to my empty cheeks.

Would you still love me even when I stop?

Ode to my Belly

Why do you growl at me in hunger,
Begging when I'm just trying to fix you?
Why are you shouting in the middle of a crowded,
sweating room
When all I'm trying to do is help you?
Don't you want to be like them?
Don't you want to be happy?
Well, don't you?

Pleading Guilty

I felt guilty
When I realised
I was taking her life away.

The little girl with chocolate brown eyes
Smiled at herself.
Because she was happy,
Because she knew she was beautiful.
Because her bare feet ran along carpeted floors
And skimming fingers painted the walls in finger prints.

I pointed at her.

"That's me." I thought
I said it out loud but she didn't hear me, or she didn't
understand.
Why would she? She was only little.
I spoke louder: "That's me!"
I shouted into her eyes and they stared through mine.

When I stopped screaming,
That's when I realised that I was still taking her life away.
That I never really gave her a life.

The little girl with chocolate brown eyes and mud-stained
knees

Lay down in my arms and cried.
I said "I'm sorry."
I screamed it at her "I'm sorry, I'm sorry, I'm sorry!"
She didn't listen, she just closed her eyes,
And let me take her tiny cold hand
In mine.

Self-portrait with an Incomplete Smile

When I was young I was told that I had a beautiful smile
When my mouth spread out far too big,
Pulling at each side of my face until my eyes were lost in cheek.
They asked me what's the trick? How am I so happy?
To tell the truth: I did not know then what I know now.

So as I sit on a reclining dentist chair,
Clinical interrogation light overhead,
I am told to open up
And so I do as I am told.
I am recommended straightened teeth,
Fuller lips and a little more proportionality.
They told me what I needed to be beautiful:
A smile that wasn't mine.

So. I look in the mirror and
Point out all the things I wish I could change
About the person I find there.
When I looked back up I noticed
My smile was incomplete.

Now, from time to time they tell me
"Cheer up" or "where did your smile go?"
I grin as if I had never known how to smile and tell them
It's closed for reconstruction, due back soon.

Singing my Part

I am not enough,
Always getting there,
Constantly in the process,
Working on it,
Trying a little too hard.

I'm tired, somehow, from standing, breathing.
It's getting hard.
And I want to cry, I really do but I can't.
Too little alcohol.

Well, now I can't breathe in.

I wonder if they know.
Even from the 20 times I told them.
In those airless rooms I want them to hurt like this
And I want it to feel as good as music.

Temperamental

Yes.
I know staring into the toilet won't make me sick
But I know I'm sick; Dr Google concurs.

No.
I thought I'd be asleep but it feels wrong; my cheeks are
making the pillow wet.

Yes.
I am glass and if you drop me and turn me pink it will be
your fault.

No.
It's nothing, sorry to disturb; it's just that everything
changes too quickly.
Do you know what I mean?

You tell me to stop over-reacting.

The Sun that Wanted to be Yellow

No one is here but me, sitting cross-legged in front of
a wall —
Intact and blindingly yellow.
A cat sits next to me, orange and ornately striped.
They see me smiling like a sweetened child.
Happiness is stretched from one side of my face
to another and
Circles of fuchsia are forced onto my cheeks.
I have become their perfection.

Yet my eyes are brown; my teeth, crooked.
My dress is torn down the middle
And, however much I ask, the seamstress refuses to fix it.
Now that I look at it again, the wall is chipped, broken
and the plaster,
Pained and punctured by fingernails.
Water is dripping down from the cracks and I can smell
rust from the metal hinges.
I am told that I am the sun - but now I'm trying too hard
to be yellow.

Weed and a Therapist

I like the crying into the bin of it,
Holding my phone screen to my heart.
I want to tell everyone.
They tell me to "shut up"
I'm spoiling the mood.
I love shouting "Weed" and "Therapist"
Like they will save me.
The hours, the stolen money.
I look in the mirror, I cry from my left eye.
That's happiness.
I fluff my pillow, hide in other lives,
I wait for tomorrow or next year, I scratch out numbers
on calendar pages,
scratch tables with pen tips and short fingernails
And splinters in my stomach.
I need the hopeless hope.
If there is a solution let it stay in the distance
Where I can only see its silhouette.

Where does the journey begin?

At the fun fair
with warped mirrors
Where someone else's body
Takes over my own.

In a café
Watching men sip
From woman shaped bottles
Rounded where I must be rounded.

Using a pediatrician's abacus
To count up numbers
That don't make sense.

Travelling with someone else's map
Losing my way and noticing
All the monuments I pass and
Reading the plaques and crying.

In a sanctuary
In the depths of Thailand. Hiding there.
A Buddhist monk starving himself in solitude
To find the in-and-out-of-fashion truth

I didn't realise how long I had left,
How long I had been gone for

Until I saw myself sitting
On a Freudian couch
Picking at the leather
Waiting for a therapist to open the door.

Printed in Great Britain
by Amazon